Your Love &

Shook

A Novella

By: Shanice B.

To Keep Up With My Latest

Release Please Sign Up To My

Mailing List Below...

www.shaniceb.com

Books By Shanice B.

KISS ME WHERE IT HURTS (1-3)
HE LOVES THE SAVAGE IN ME: A TWISTED LOVE
AFFAIR (1-2)
LOVE, I THOUGHT YOU HAD MY BACK
(STANDALONE)
MARRIED TO A DEKALB COUNTY BULLY
(STANDALONE)
ALL I EVER WANTED WAS YOU: A TWISTED LOVE
STORY (1-2)
FEENIN' FOR THAT DOPE DICK (AN EROTIC SHORT
STORY)
NO ONE HAS TO KNOW: A SECRET WORTH KEEPING
MEET ME IN MY BEDROOM: A COLLECTION OF
EROTIC LOVE STORIES (VOLUME 1&2)
ALL I NEED IS YOU: A CHRISTMAS LOVE STORY
(STANDALONE)
I WISH YOU WERE MY BOO: A TRAGIC LOVE STORY
(STANDALONE

Love is giving someone the power to destroy you and trusting them not to.

Prologue

Yvonne

A Week Earlier

My pussy was dripping with anticipation as Ricco unzipped my skin-tight jeans and pulled them off my round ass. I bit down on my bottom lip as he kissed me gently on my neck.

"Damn, you smell so fucking good," he whispered into my ear.

I stared into his beautiful brown eyes as he tore off the rest of my clothes and slid between my thighs.

I squeezed my eyes shut as he started sucking on my pussy.

"Fuck," I cried out as he worked his magic with his tongue.

It wasn't long before I reached a mind-blowing orgasm that had my legs shaking.

Ricco licked up every drop of my sweet nectar before sliding his tongue deep into my mouth. He broke the kiss a few moments later and started trailing kisses from my lips all the way down to my toes.

Ricco knew exactly what to do to turn me on. I was so wet that he could have easily dived in at that very moment.

After he had made love to my toes, he pulled his shorts down and began stroking his manhood.

He didn't even have to tell me he wanted his dick sucked, I already knew what to do. I sat on the edge of the bed and slid his thick pole into my hot mouth. I made sure to also play with his balls as I deep throated his dick.

"Shit baby," he said softly as he rubbed his hands through my long burgundy dreads.

Whenever I sucked him off, I always made sure to suck him until his soul left his body. Just when he was about to, he pulled his manhood from my mouth, and pushed me down on the bed. I opened my chocolate colored thighs and wrapped them around his waist as he slid deep into my honey pot.

"I love you," he whispered into my ear as he licked my ear and pulled my hair.

He started out giving me slow deep strokes until I was begging him to fuck me harder. I squeezed my eyes shut and were near tears when he bent my legs over my head.

"Shit!" I yelled out as I tried to push him out of me.

"Nall, you said you wanted me to fuck you harder. You going to take this damn dick tonight," he growled at me.

When my pussy began to paint his dick with white cream, he pulled out of my wetness and flipped me over.

"Ass up," he instructed me.

I grabbed a pillow and buried my face into it as he gave me some back shots.

"Yes, right their baby, arch that fucking back. Give me that fucking pussy."

When he pulled his tool out of me and started eating my ass, I almost fell over. The shit was feeling too damn good.

Ricco held me firmly as he flicked his tongue around my booty hole before sliding a finger inside.

I felt as if I was on a fucking high and I wasn't anywhere near ready to come down from it. As he ate my ass like it was a late-night snack, I played with my clit and was near reaching another climax when he grabbed the lube from my nightstand and began to massage my asshole. I already knew what he had planned, and I wasn't sure if I was down with it. Ricco immediately sensed my hesitation and told me to calm down.

"Baby, just relax," he told me just as he placed a kiss on my lips.

When he slid his ten inches into my ass, I tried to run, but this nigga grabbed me by my waist."

"Shhhhh, I only put the head in. I just wanted to try something different, stay calm I'm not trying to hurt you."

I counted to ten, relaxed my ass muscles, and buried my face back into the pillow as he gently began to stroke his love stick inside of me. Just as he had promised the pain finally subsided as he played with my clit, with his hand.

I let out a moan which made Ricco chuckle.

"See, I told you, that you were going to like it. You want me to go deeper?" he asked as I began to twerk my ass on his dick.

"Yes baby, go a little deeper."

As he went deeper, I continued to rub on my clit until I started squirting.

"Oooohhhhh shit baby, I'm about to cum," Ricco, groaned as he yanked me by my hair.

"Cum for me daddy, fill this ass hole up with your cum."

When Ricco busted his nut, I busted right along with him.

He pulled his manhood out of me a few seconds later and we both grabbed us a cigarette.

We sat in bed and smoked as we both talked about our day. I was literally drained, but I didn't want to fall asleep just yet. After I had put my cigarette out, I laid down on Ricco's chest and rubbed my hands up and down his almond colored skin.

I was crazy in love with Ricco and was addicted to him. No matter how hard I tried, I could never get enough of him. Not only was he sexy as hell but the nigga had shit going for himself. He was only thirty years old and had already worked his way up as the

General Manager at Best Buy. I was super proud of my man and his accomplishments but hated all the attention that he received from these thirsty ass bitches.

Ricco was tall, muscular, almond in complexion, with straight white teeth, he rocked a low cut with his sides faded, and rocked a thick black beard that he kept neatly trimmed. He could pull any bitch that he wanted with just his looks alone. Standing in the shadows there was always some hoe that was eager to please.

When Ricco and I first met two years ago, I knew from the moment that we set eyes on each other that Ricco wanted me as much as I wanted him. The sexual chemistry that we had for one another was mind-blowing.

It was on a cold windy day in October when I met Ricco. I just happened to be at Starbucks ordering my usual latte when we bumped into each other. I was running late for work and wasn't watching where I was going. I bumped into him and dropped my latte on the floor spilling it everywhere. He apologized, to me a million times before offering me a new cup of coffee. From that day forward Rico and had been inseparable.

"Baby, I hope you know I love you," Ricco muttered.

"You would be dumb not to love me," I joked.

Ricco chuckled.

He placed a kiss on my head and caressed my arm with his finger.

Just when sleep was about to find me, I heard Ricco's phone vibrating. He reached over to retrieve it, but didn't answer the bitch, instead, he sent whoever it was to voicemail.

"Who was that?" I asked him suspiciously.

I mean I was curious to know who was calling his ass at almost one in the morning.

"It wasn't nobody important baby, gone and close your eyes, you have to get up in the morning."

I was way too tired to stress over a dumb ass phone call, but the fact that this nigga didn't have friends was what started me having all these questions pop up in my mind.

I knew in my heart it wasn't a nigga hitting him up this fucking late, but I prayed for his own safety that it wasn't a bitch. I stayed ready to fuck a nigga up. Yes, I loved Ricco with all my heart, but just because I loved him didn't mean I was stupid in love for his ass.

I was in the middle of pouring drinks when my homegirl Bambi tapped me on my shoulder.

"Bitch, we need to talk when you get a minute."

"About what?" I asked her quizzically.

"I got some shit to tell you that is going to blow your mind."

Just when I was about to ask her to explain she walked off to take someone's drink order. I wasn't going to drive myself crazy tonight trying to figure out what Bambi had to tell me that would blow my mind. Instead, I got busy with wiping down the bar.

I had only been to work for an hour and I was counting down the time that I could dip the fuck out and head back home. I didn't want to be here, but I couldn't sit home on my ass thinking that I was going to get paid.

At night, I was a bartender and during the day I did hair. I was working two jobs, even though my man of two years always stressed to me that I didn't have to do any of it.

I was raised to be independent and take care of my own. I never wanted a nigga to fix his lips to talk about what he had to do for me.

I was on my shit and wasn't about to let a nigga sweet talk me into believing that he could make things easier for me by letting him take care of me. My mother didn't raise a weak ass bitch, I learned from her to never depend on a nigga for shit.

I was exhausted from not being able to get all my beauty sleep. After being at the Hair Salon all morning, I came home thinking I was going to get in bed, but sleep was the last thing I was going to be getting. I came home to find my boo, Ricco naked in our

King-sized bed. He was laying there watching a flick and stroking

his dick. I wasn't about to let my nigga masturbate to some other

bitch. I hurried to undress and gave him exactly what he needed.

I fucked Ricco for an hour straight before I finally was able to

rest my eyes for work later that night. Even though Ricco begged

for me to stay home, I left and came to work because I needed all

the money I could get. I loved stacking my own coins and I wasn't

about to stop my hustle for no nigga.

Even though Ricco complained that I worked a lot and didn't

have to, I secretly felt like he loved that quality about me. He

didn't have to worry about taking care of me or stressing out about

what I was going to do if we ever went our separate ways.

A bitch was smarter than that, I didn't want to trap any nigga,

because I didn't want anyone trapping me. We had the perfect

relationship and I was extremely happy with my man. We were

living together and vibing very good. I knew in my heart that it wasn't going to be long before he got down on bended knee and asked me to marry him, just the thought of me spending the rest of my life with the man I love filled my heart with warmth.

Before I met Ricco, I never thought that I was ever going to find the right man for me. It seemed as if I kept choosing niggas who didn't want shit and didn't want me to have shit either. I wanted to break free, I wanted money and success, the men before him didn't feel the same. Ricco came into my life when I least expected it and showed me what a real man truly was. I had upgraded from fucking around with little boys to falling in love with a grown man who wanted shit from life.

Ricco wasn't just laying around all day, eating cereal, and playing video games. He wasn't the type of nigga to let life ass fuck him and take all his dreams. Ricco drive was phenomenal and sparked something in my soul. There wasn't any other nigga that could get my attention and make me want to fuck up what we had going on.

I was sexy as hell and with working at a bar late at night, there was plenty of men who tried to run game on my ass, but I knew what I had at home and I wasn't about to fuck that shit up for nothing in the world.

I rolled my eyes as a nigga took a seat in front of me and started trying to flirt.

A bitch was tired and wasn't in the mood for a nigga to be all up in my face.

"Damn, your ass sure is pretty, can I have your number boo?"

I laughed at his ass.

Niggas came in here every night trying to flirt with me. All they saw was a pretty face and fat ass and was fascinated over just that. I sized the nigga up who had just asked for my number and knew immediately he was just like all the rest of the niggas who came in here trying to pull a bad bitch.

"Thanks for the compliment, but I belong to someone."

The nigga was sexy as hell, I couldn't deny that shit. He was light in complexion, long dreads, thick juicy lips, with a stud in his nose, he had dark brown eyes that were watching me as I wiped down his area that he was sitting at.

"What can I get for you?" I asked.

"A Coors Light will do."

I popped open his beer, grabbed a mat from behind the counter, and placed it under his beer.

I was just about to head over to serve another customer when he asked me what my name was.

"Yvonne," I told him as I stared into his piercing eyes.

"Yvonne, can I at least get your number."

I leaned over the counter to look at him more closely. I guess he thought I was going to be like all these other basic bitches and let him fuck, but that wasn't me. I wasn't about to even entertain his ass.

"I'm not about to give you my number. Like I just told you, I have someone. I'm loyal to my nigga."

The nigga smirked at me.

"What your nigga don't know won't hurt him. Just because you faithful to that nigga don't mean he faithful to you."

"That's where you're wrong. I can trust my nigga."

"Nobody can be trusted these days, not even your nigga, believe that shorty."

I rolled my eyes at him and walked away to serve my next customer. I honestly didn't have time for his bullshit.

Things finally began to slow down an hour later. It was Friday night, so bitches and niggas stayed ready to get fucked up.

Bambi walked over to me a few moments later and slapped me on the ass.

"Damn bitch, that shit hurt," I told her as she laughed at my reaction.

"That big ass you got back there, you ain't even feel that shit."

Bambi leaned over me as I was stacking the glasses on top of one another and whispered into my ear.

"I need to talk to you about Ricco."

I stopped what I was doing and gave her my full attention.

She grabbed me by my hand and we headed into the back so we could have a little privacy. My feet felt heavy as I followed Bambi to where we kept the rest of the liquor stored.

I found some shit out yesterday about Ricco. I know you gonna wonder why I didn't tell you right then when I saw the shit, but I just couldn't. I had to make sure that I had all the facts before I stepped to you with this shit.

"What the fuck are you talking about?" I asked Bambi.

Bambi took a deep breath and spilled the tea on Ricco.

"Yesterday morning, I spotted Ricco coming out of Starbucks."

"And…"

"And he wasn't alone. He was with some other bitch that wasn't you. They were hugged up together."

I felt as if I had been slapped. This couldn't be true. I began to pray that Bambi was going to burst out laughing that she was only fucking with me, but as I stared at her I knew she was serious about this shit.

I grabbed a chair and took a seat as Bambi continued to tell me what she had witnessed.

"You know the type of bitch I am. I wasn't going to just turn my head to the bullshit."

What did you do? I asked hoarsely.

"I followed his ass."

I nearly had a heart attack. I swear Bambi, was the type of bitch who didn't give a fuck about anything. She was solid as hell and I loved her ass for it. She had always been down for me and always looked out for me when I was too naïve and in love with my nigga to peep game.

"Don't sit there and looked shocked, you know I got your back boo. Anyway, I followed his ass and bam, I pull up at these apartments on the Northside. I sat there for a few moments and waited for them to get out of the car. When they finally hopped out, Ricco pushed the little bitch up against his car and stuck his tongue down her throat.

Tears began to pour down my face because never could I imagine Ricco cheating on me with anyone.

"Who is the bitch?" I asked Bambi angrily.

"I ain't never seen the hoe before, but she looks younger than us. If I had to guess I would say the bitch about twenty."

As I continued to listen to Bambi tears began to pour down my face. I was an emotional wreck, my heart felt like it had been shattered.

Bambi walked over to me and embraced me in a tight hug as she tried to console me.

"Don't do this. Please, don't cry over that fuck nigga, you better than this."

"I just can't believe, he would do this to me."

"I know what you mean, I honestly didn't think that Ricco was that type of nigga, but apparently, he fooled us both."

"Did you get a picture or video?" I asked Bambi as she held me.

"No, I didn't get a chance to get one boo, you just got to trust me on this. Do you trust me?"

"Yes, I trust you with my life," I cried on her.

Bambi pulled away from me a few moments later and wiped the tears from my eyes.

The vibration of my phone let me knew that someone was trying to call me. I handed the phone to Bambi when I saw that it was Ricco. There was no way in hell I was going to be able to talk to him without crying.

I closed my eyes and listened to Bambi as she talked with Ricco for a few moments. When she hung up the phone, I asked her what he wanted.

"He told me to tell you that he going to hang out with his boys tonight and not wait up for him."

"Wow, he probably going to lay up with that bitch," I replied bitterly.

"Exactly. So, what we going to do is clock the fuck out and do a drive by just to see if he going to be at this hoe house. Our shift is over, Richard and Candace should be clocking in at any second," Bambi assured me.

I wiped the last of my tears from my eyes and hopped off the chair. I was done crying and trying to figure out why Ricco had betrayed me. It was time to fuck some shit up. Ricco was about to find out that he had chosen the wrong bitch to cheat on.

Chapter 2

Lyanne

"Don't worry about taking your car, just hop in mine. I'm going to bring you back to pick your car up when we get through taking care of this situation," Bambi told as we headed out the bar.

I hopped into Bambi's 2006 all black Altima and clicked my seat belt into place. I held on to my fucking seat as Bambi weaved in and out of traffic.

I pulled out my phone and tried to call Ricco, but his phone went straight to voicemail. I was super pissed because this only made me think that he was laid up with some other bitch. This nigga never cut his phone off, so I knew he was on some fuck shit.

Twenty minutes later Bambi and I were on the Northside of Warner Robins. We rode around for a good minute before we spotted Ricco's Dodge Charger at the Northside Garden Apartment Complex. Bambi pulled up beside his car and we hopped out. I was ready to fuck some shit up and was hoping a bitch would say some foul shit to me.

"Which apartment?" I asked Bambi crossly.

Bambi pointed to the apartment that was only a few feet away. I walked my ass towards the door and knocked on that bitch.

(Rich The Kid-Small Things) blasted from behind the door so I knew that my knock probably went unheard. I knocked harder, but still, nobody came to the fucking door. I picked up a rock that was laying on the ground walked over to where I assumed the living room was at and threw the rock through the fucking window.

"Ricco, are you in there? Bring your bitch as outside now."

The glass shattered and I snatched the curtains out of my way to find Ricco deep inside the very bitch that Bambi had described. I swear the whole room started spinning and I lost all control.

Ricco pushed the bitch off him, but it was little too late for that shit.

"Who the fuck is you? I'm calling the fucking police, your ass is fucking crazy, you just smashed a brick through my fucking window!" the little hoe yelled with attitude.

"Bitch, if you don't shut the fuck up. I'm Ricco's bitch, oh he didn't tell you about me?" I asked her nastily.

"Yeah, I bet that bitch know he got somebody," Bambi replied.

"Yeah, I bet your ass ain't innocent in this fucking situation," I spat at Ricco's lil' hoe.

"Get the fuck out of my shit before I call the law," she yelled at me.

I was just about to go into attack mode and beat the bitch down but my bitch Bambi beat me to it. She smacked the bitch across her face so hard the hoe fell to the floor.

"Shut the fuck up hoe, sit the fuck down, you ain't about to call nobody, try me if you want to, I will knock all them teeth out your fucking throat," Bambi spat.

I swear Bambi was the perfect bitch to bring with me when I had to handle some real shit, the bitch was ruthless and stayed ready to bust a bitch in her face.

I turned my attention towards Ricco who had been hurrying to get dressed the whole entire time that his little bitch was trying to run her mouth.

"You honestly thought I wasn't going to find out about you fucking up on me. Nigga I been rocking with your ass for two fucking years and this how you going to do me? I ain't been nothing but loyal to you and here you are fucking a young ass bitch who barely out of high school. You up here robbing the fucking

cradle bitch, you going to cheat on a boss ass bitch like myself for

this hoe who can barely probably write her damn name, the bitch

still drinking Similac. I'm twenty-nine years old nigga, I'm a

grown ass bitch, and you want this hoe? I asked him as I point to

the young bitch.

"Baby, it isn't nothing serious. It don't mean shit, I'm sorry

baby," Ricco stuttered.

"What the fuck Ricco? You told me you were going to leave the

bitch!" the hoe shouted at him with attitude.

I stood there as if my heart had been snatched out my chest.

Ricco looked over at the young bitch and gave her that facial

expression to tell her to shut the hell up, but it was too late. I had

already lost all ounce of self-control that I had. I didn't think twice

about picking up the rock that I had thrown inside the house and

throwing it directly at his dome.

Loud screaming broke out and that's when the fighting began. Ricco laid stretched out on the damn floor crying out in pain as the rock popped him across the head.

I walked over to him kicked him in his stomach and back with as much force as I could. I wanted to kill the fuck nigga and I probably would have done that shit if Bambi and his side bitch wouldn't have pushed me away from him with their fighting.

Just that split second of getting away from his dumb ass saved his life. Blood seeped from his mouth as he stared up at me.

"You fucked with the wrong bitch," I whispered to him.

I walked away from him at that very moment because I didn't want to do some shit that I later regretted. Instead of smashing his face in with the rock, I took my anger out towards his side bitch crib. I smashed her flat screen tv, smashed her fucking tables and chairs, smashed all her windows out her crib, and pulled out my pocket knife that I carried with me for protection and sliced up her furniture.

The fact that this bitch knew about me was what fueled my anger towards her, even though Bambi was dragging her ass I wanted to make sure that I got me some licks in too. She was going to learn about fucking around with another bitch's nigga.

I dragged her by her weave and punched her in her face until I had busted her nose. I slammed her head on the floor a few times before Bambi pulled me off her.

"Yvonne, we got to get the fuck out of here the police are on the way."

I could hear the sirens in the distance, so I knew they were going to be here soon. We needed to get the fuck out of there because if we were there when they pulled up, we were going to be spending the night in jail.

I stomped the bitch one good time before Bambi and I left.

I walked over to Ricco's all black Dodge Charger and scraped it from the front to the back with my pocket knife.

Bambi and I hopped into her car and pulled out of Northside Gardens with our music blasting **(Keke Palmer-Bossy).** I didn't give a fuck about what we had done or that the police were on their way. If you asked me, Ricco and his little side piece needed that ass whooping that Bambi and I had just given them.

Bambi turned the music down a few moments later and looked over at me.

"Are you good over there?"

"I'm good, I just can't believe Ricco played me the way he did."

"I didn't know he was that fucking dumb, but apparently," he is, Bambi muttered

"I already know that little scary ass bitch going to file charges," I replied.

"Nah, you ain't got to worry about that, I got a homeboy who married to a police officer. All I got to do is give him a call and all this shit will be swept under the rug."

"Well, damn bitch, it looks like you got everything taken care of,"

Bambi laughed.

"We are not about to go to jail for beating a bitch ass. I'm all for the fuckery you know that," Bambi replied.

I already knew that Bambi wasn't lying, she was always down to knock a bitch out if they ever got wrong with either one of us. Even though I had a loyal friend on my side who would stick by me and never hurt me, my heart still felt empty. Ricco had torn my heart to pieces, and I had no way of knowing if I ever was going to be the same ever again.

Chapter 3

Yvonne

The Next Morning

Instead of going to work like I did every morning, I got up and started packing up all Ricco's shit. I didn't want anything in my apartment that belonged to his ass. I grabbed a big ass box that I found from the laundry room and began to throw some of his shoes and clothes in it until it was filled up. I dragged it down the hallway towards the front door and went back to work in my room. I cleaned out my entire closet and made sure every little shred of clothing shoes, hats, and jackets were out. After the closet was clean, I headed over to his nightstand and pulled out some more of his shit and threw them in a Glad bag before heading over to his dressers where he kept his boxers, socks, and belts. I emptied all three dressers and tied the Glad trash bag and started on the bathroom. I grabbed all his personal items such as his toothbrush, toothpaste, shaving cream etc, and threw them in another bag and tied it. I dragged the bags all the way outside and sat them bitches on the front porch. I didn't even want his ass coming into my apartment, I wanted him to stay far away from me. I was so angry that I didn't want to end up doing some crazy shit that would lead me to serve a life sentence.

I pulled out my phone and took a picture of his shit outside in garbage bags and told him to come get it or I was going to sell everything. I wasn't playing with this nigga. He was going to learn today that I wasn't the bitch to fuck with.

Twenty minutes later, I heard someone beating at my door. I headed towards the kitchen grabbed a knife out the kitchen drawer and went back to the living room. I opened the door and there stood Ricco, looking at me with pleading eyes.

"Baby, I'm sorry, please forgive me, you ain't got to put me out. We can get through this."

He tried stepping into the apartment, but I pointed my knife at him.

"Don't come any farther. Get your shit and get the fuck off my property. Nigga, I gave you my all and you didn't do shit with it but fuck it all up for some other bitch. I hope that little young pussy was worth it," I spat at him.

"I admit, I fucked up, but I don't want her."

I laughed because the shit was comical to me.

"Nigga, don't come over here lying to me. You told that bitch you were going to leave me for her, so do what you said. We are over, it's no coming back from this."

"It was as if he wasn't getting anything that I was saying because this nigga was still at my doorstep trying to plead his case."

"You really got me wondering about you, how can you cut me off like this and not give me a second chance? You didn't love me anyway!" he yelled at me.

I chuckled. This nigga was trying to flip shit on me like I was the problem. One thing I hated more than a liar was a manipulative ass nigga.

"What you fail to realize is, I do love you, but I love myself more. I'm not taking you back because I'm not going to ever allow your ass to fuck me over again. Once a cheater is always a damn cheater, if you can do it once, you can do it again, maybe not with her ass, but there will be some other bitch, you going to want to smash and yet again, I will be the one looking stupid. Nope, not this time, you had your chance, you fucked up, now get your shit and bounce."

He stared at me for a while, as if he was in deep thought. A few moments later, he grabbed his things and headed to the car. I guess he must have thought about what I had just told him, he probably knew that he was eventually going to be tempted again to cheat. I wanted him away from me because the next time he fucked up I wasn't going to show his ass any mercy.

He had fucked over a good bitch and thought he was going to continue to get away with it. My girl Bambi was at the right place at the right fucking time, because if she wouldn't have never spotted Ricco with his little side piece, I would be sitting here in the fucking dark and being made a fool of.

Instead of crying and moping around for the rest of the day, I took a shower and got dressed. My phone started going off and I answered when I saw that it was Bambi calling me.

"Are you up?"

"Yeah, I'm up. I just finished getting dressed."

"Good, because I'm about to swoop by and pick your ass up. I'm taking you out."

"Where are we going?"

"Look at you, you so fucking nosy," Bambi joked.

"Shid, I need to know where you're taking my ass," I laughed.

"I'm taking you out to eat, are you happy now?"

"I'm very happy. I'm about to pull up in a few so be outside."

I glossed my lips with a little gloss, pulled my dreads back in a ponytail and headed out the door.

Bambi pulled up and I hopped my ass inside.

"You good boo?"

"Yeah, I'm good. Ricco came by not too long ago."

"Let me guess, he tried to sweet talk you into taking him back."

"Bitch, you already know he did. I already had all his shit packed up outside. I'm good on him. I told him to kick rocks."

"You did the right thing boo. I know it hurts like hell, but I'm here for you."

"It does hurt, but I'm a strong ass bitch, I will get over it."

"Niggas just don't know when they have a good thing," Bambi added.

"You right, but Ricco knew exactly what he had, he just wanted extra pussy on the side. I don't get down like that. I'm not about to accept that shit from no nigga."

"You don't deserve that," Bambi replied gently.

I only nodded my head as I stared out the window.

A heartbreak was hard to get over. There wasn't any such thing as a time limit of when your heart should stop hurting, even though friends, family, and doctors wanted it to be a quick process, it never was. I had been single for over two years due to the fact of me not wanting to give my all to a bitch only for her to fuck me over. My heart was still filled with anger every time I thought back to my last girlfriend who had made a complete fool of me. She had hurt me to my core, and I feared that I probably never was going to recover. Imagine being with someone for over five years to learn that they were living a double life, imagine coming home one day to find the person you love gone with only a letter telling you that the relationship has been dead for a very long time. I had worked

my ass off the entire time for her to up and leave me for a nigga

who didn't have shit. She was practically taking care of her new

man with the money that I had busted my ass to earn. I couldn't

wrap my mind around how she could leave without a dollar to her

name. She didn't work and she didn't have her own money. I was

the provider and told her that I was going to take care of her. I

didn't mind, I wanted my Queen to stay home stress-free. When

she left abruptly with only a detailed letter saying we were over, I

did a little digging myself and found out that this bitch had a whole

account that I didn't know about and had been stashing away

money the entire time she had been with me. I had been with

Karmen for five years and didn't know that I was sleeping with the

enemy. With a little investigation work, I found out where that

little hoe ran off to. I wanted to contact her just so I could have

closure. I wanted to know why she had fucked me over the way she did, but decided to leave her ass alone. Deep in my heart, I already knew that there was no love there in her heart for me, and there never was. I was blinded by what I wanted her to be when I should have seen her for what she truly was.

Just to know that the bitch I had given my all had run off with an ex-con who I later found out was her high school sweetheart floored me. I had been her rebound until the man she truly loved had done his time and was free again. After going through the humiliation of being used, I made myself a promise to never fall in love again and so far for the past two years I had kept that promise to myself.

I fucked a lot of bitches, but I wasn't trying to go beyond that point. All I wanted was a quick nut, I didn't have any love for any of the bitches I fucked. My heart was cold and it was going to stay that way.

I had other shit that I needed to be focused on. I was the CEO of Omari's realtor company. I sold houses to the middle-class citizens of Warner Robins and was the top realtor company around. My company was just getting off the ground when Karmen up and left my ass, but now two years later, I had a whole staff team. I also had positions that The staff worked hard and in return, I made sure to look out for each of them. Running a business was hard work and took dedication and patience. I wanted so much out of life and was willing to bust my ass to get it. A relationship was last on my list, I was focused on building my empire. The only thing that I had been loyal to me was my career. I found comfort in my heart, knowing that I would never wake up to learn that my career didn't love me anymore. Putting love first was bound to fuck anyone up in the long run.

A knock at my door pulled me from my thoughts.

"Come in," I said.

"Mr. Henderson, I have great news, Mr. Garry is on the line and is interested in sealing the deal for the five-bedroom four-bedroom home in Kathleen," Kay informed me.

Kay had been my assistant since I first started my own realtor company. She was a beautiful dark chocolate black woman who probably could pull any nigga that she wanted. She was petite in size, with big beautiful eyes, with long dark hair that stopped at her ass. I was very much attracted to her, but I always remained professional since she was married.

I didn't want to get myself caught up in any drama. I could tell by how Kay looked at me that she wanted to get a sample of this dick, but neither one of us dared to cross the line. It seemed like she had the perfect marriage. Her husband brought her lunch every day, attended all her job functions with her, and treated her like the black Queen that she was.

Kay and her husband were lucky to find each other, I just hated that I haven't been so lucky. It wasn't anything wrong with looking and admiring other people and that's what Kay did. She admired me and probably even fantasized about me, but it wasn't going to go any farther than that.

"Thank you, Kay, which line is Mr. Garry on?"

"Line 2," Kay replied excitedly.

I already knew why she was so happy, whenever we sold a half a million-dollar home I always made sure to give everyone who worked in my office a raise, even the janitors were given one as well.

I talked to Mr. Garry for about ten minutes before he rushed me off the phone because he had to see about one of his patients, but just before the call ended, he assured me that he was going to stop by later that day to sign his name on the dotted line. I got off the phone a few moments later with my heart racing.

I immediately called a meeting in the conference room and waited patiently for the twenty realtors that I had on my team to take a seat.

"There are no secrets in this building, so I already know that everyone may have heard the good news about the surgeon Mr. Garry is interested in signing for the half a million-dollar property in Kathleen. I just got off the phone with him and he reassured me that he will be coming by after work to sign on the dotted line."

Everyone started cheering and hi-fiving one another. After everyone had settled down, I continued to finish what I had come there to say.

"If you got plans for later today cancel them because we are celebrating. After the deal has been signed, I'm taking everyone to the bar and buying drinks."

"That sounds like a plan boss man!" Jimmy yelled out from the back.

"Okay, get back to work, and make me proud."

Everyone filed out of the conference room with happy smiles on their faces.

I headed out of the conference room last and was almost to my office when I spotted Brandy. Brandy had been interning with me for about two weeks. She was attending Central Georgia Technical College for business and was top of her class. She was only nineteen years old, caramel in complexion, slim, medium in height, with shoulder-length hair. She had brown hazel eyes, straight white teeth, and juicy fat lips. She was fine as hell and no matter how hard I tried I couldn't stop looking at her.

Today she was dressed in a pair of black shorts, a white top, with a pair of white and black sandals. Her hair was pulled back in a ponytail and her juicy lips were painted with some hot pink lipstick.

I walked over to her and told her to follow me into my office. I closed the door behind us and took a seat behind my desk. She took a seat in a chair in front of my desk and crossed her legs.

"I know you haven't been here long, but everyone is heading to the bar tonight in celebration of a deal that is going to be signed for a half a million-dollar home. If you don't have plans for tonight, you can tag along. Everyone in the office will be attending even the cleanup crew."

Brandy eyes sparkled as she leaned over my desk. I tried avoiding staring at her titties, but it was hard to do. They were looking big and juicy.

"I will love to come. I have no plans," Brandy told me as she stared at me.

"Perfect, all drinks on me tonight, so come and have a great time.

Of course, that's the plan when your boss is buying drinks," Brandy joked.

"How are you liking interning here? Do you believe this is something you would be interested in?" I asked her professionally.

Brandy smiled and that's when I noticed she had dimples in her cheek.

"I love it here, I've learned so much," she commented.

I listened as she started talking about her future after college. I was very impressed because her goals were mind-blowing.

After talking to her for over twenty minutes, I pulled out her internship paper and made sure to mark an A on her grade sheet. Every week I always had to send a report back to her professor to let her know how Brandy had worked that week.

These past two weeks she had been to work on time and had done everything that was asked of her. No one in the office had any complaints on her so that was a relief.

After filling out her paperwork I placed it on the other side of my desk and talked to her a little bit longer. As she continued to talk, I continued to check her out without her knowing.

After a while, she started to notice that I was undressing her with her eyes because she stood up and walked over to me. I didn't move and I didn't dare touch her. I always wanted to keep business and pleasure separate, I never fucked around with anyone who worked for me since shit could go left at any time. I guess Brandy must have noticed my hesitation because she wasted no time bending over and whispering in my ear that she didn't work for me.

"No one has to know about this, whatever happens, is only between us. I know you want me and I would be lying if I said I didn't want you."

Her perfume filled my nose as she began to lick around my ear lobe. My manhood felt as if it was about to burst out my pants.

Brandy knew exactly what she doing to me.

"Touch me, Mr. Henderson," she cooed in my ear.

As hard as I wanted to fight it I couldn't. Next thing you know my hands were caressing her tight firm body. I massaged her ass with my hand just before pulling her on top of my lap. Our lips connected and our tongues danced in each other mouths. We kissed for the longest moment before she pulled away from me.

"We don't have much time before someone comes knocking at your door," she told me as she zipped my pants down and pulled my dick out.

She licked her lips before getting down on her knees and licking the tip of my head.

"Fuck," I choked out.

I closed my eyes and let her did her thing. She sucked and slurped on my dick like she was a porn star. I rubbed my hands through her shoulder length hair as she tried to snatch my soul.

She pulled my manhood out of my mouth, spit on it and slurped it up before deep throating me. This little bitch wasn't anything but nineteen but knew how to suck dick better than a bitch in their thirties.

"I'm about to bust," I told her.

Brandy continued to suck and grip my dick like she ain't heard me. A few seconds later I spilled my seed down her throat. She sucked me dry and stood up like it was something that she did on a regular basis. I slid my dick back into my pants while she finger-combed her hair.

"See you tonight Mr. Henderson," Brandy told me before walking out of my office.

I sat there still not being able to grasp what had just happened to me.

Chapter

Three

Later that Evening

After Mr. Garry had signed his name on the dotted line, we shook hands, and I passed him the key to his new home. When he was well out of sight and had left out of my office only then did I make the announcement that had everyone cheering.

"Is everyone one ready to celebrate tonight at Snappers Lounge?"

"Hell yeah!" everyone yelled out.

After everyone had grabbed their things, we all headed out of the office towards our cars.

Five minutes later I was pulling up at Snappers Lounge and hopped out my car. Some of the employees pulled up beside me and we all headed inside.

The bar wasn't really crowded which was good, I wanted to make sure we had enough room for everyone to enjoy themselves. I took a seat in front of the bar and waited for someone to take my drink order. As I waited, I chatted with a few employees until a woman walked over and asked what I wanted to drink.

For a moment, I couldn't speak. Her beauty was overwhelming. She was medium in height, milk chocolate in complexion, thick in all the right places, and was rocking some long burgundy dreads. I looked into her eyes and saw nothing but pain behind them. I knew instantly that she had been hurt and it probably had something to do with a nigga.

"Um, did you hear me? Can I have your drink order?" she asked

impatiently.

I smiled at her and told her that I was buying a shot for my

employees.

"How many drinks do you need?" she asked nonchalantly.

"About sixty shots will do and if they order anything else just put

it on one bill."

"Coming right up."

As she busied herself behind the counter making our drinks, the

rest of my employees came inside and found them somewhere to

sit close by. Everyone laughed and joked around while I continued

to stare at the beauty behind the counter.

"What's your name beautiful?"

She stopped what she was doing and eyed me up.

"Don't come up in here thinking you about to shoot your shot with me, it isn't about to happen. You don't need to know my name," she said with attitude.

Damn, the lil' bitch had just chewed my ass out, but it was all good. I loved the fact that she was feisty. She intrigued me even more.

I don't see a ring on your finger, so I assume you ain't married.

She rolled her eyes as she passed me my shot. My employees stood up and grabbed their drinks as well and went back to where they were sitting.

"You too damn beautiful to be having such a funky attitude."

"Look, I'm not in the mood tonight. It's been a long fucking day. I'm supposed to be home sleep in my fucking bed, but I'm here because someone called in sick."

I raised my hand up to let her know that I didn't mean to offend her.

"What shift do you normally work?" I asked her curiously.

I peeped game real quick, the fact that she didn't want me trying to flirt with her, I decided to switch it up and let her do the talking. And I had finally hit on something, she wanted to talk about work, and I was the man to listen.

She stopped what she was doing and stared at me.

"Why you want to know what shift I work?" she asked me curiously.

"I'm just curious. I come in here a few times a month in the evening and I have never seen you on this shift."

She shook her head at me as she bit down on her lip.

"I don't ever work evening shifts, my shift, is late night."

"I see, well can I at least get your name so I can tell your supervisor just how good you mixed my drink."

My heart skipped a beat when I finally saw her eyes lit up and a smile on her face.

"You have such a pretty smile, you really should smile more often."

"Do you always come in bars and try to run game on the bartenders?"

"Hell to no, I ain't met a bartender that looks like you. You are gorgeous."

"Thank you," she muttered.

I was just about to talk to her a little more when someone tapped me on the shower.

"Sorry boss that I'm late, I had a situation that I had to deal with."

My body stiffened when I noticed that it was Brandy. She took a seat next to me and asked if I was going to buy her a drink.

"Sure," I told her.

"Can I have another shot?" I asked the sexy bartender

She nodded her head as she poured Brandy a shot. I passed Brandy her drink and sat their sort of uncomfortable. I could feel the bartender staring at Brandy and me, but I didn't know exactly what to do. Here I was trying to shoot my shot at the bartender and here Brandy was nearly begging for my attention. Getting head from Brandy was the wrong fucking move because I should have known she was going to feel some type of way if I brushed her off. I mean damn, I wanted to get to know the bartender, but I had Brandy sitting next to me, this was awkward as fuck.

Brandy was far from dumb and after I didn't show her any interest that I wanted to flirt with her or even talk to her, she got up and whispered into my ear, "see you at work boss man, have fun with your little bitch tonight."

I wasn't expecting Brandy to say any of that shit, I stood up and pulled her to the side just so no one wouldn't hear our conversation.

"What the fuck is wrong with you?" I spat at her.

"Ain't shit wrong with me. I'm Gucci over here Mr. Henderson. It just funny how you can be all into me earlier today and practically undressing the fucking bartender a few hours later. I already see what type of nigga you are. You ain't trying to be serious or cuff no bitch, you just looking for a quick nut. I know that I may be your intern and not fully work for you, but do me a favor, don't look at me and never touch me again. I thought what we did back there in your office was going to lead us to at least being fuck buddies. I know most niggas like you don't like being tied down in no relationship, but damn I wouldn't have thought you would have hopped to the next bitch this fast."

"Brandy, what you and I did, was…"

"Was what? It was just a rush you had? You had a fucking urge to nut and decided to use me?"

"Brandy look, will you please calm down, don't make a fucking scene."

Brandy laughed.

"I'm not making a scene, I'm just irritated. All ya'll men are alike. Always trying to stick ya'll dick into something."

"You don't fucking know me, you don't know what I've been through," I told her crossly.

Brandy smirked.

"And you don't know me either or what I'm capable of doing."

"Are you threatening me?" I asked her angrily

Brandy snickered.

"Nigga, don't flatter yourself. I'm not going to carry on with this conversation any longer, go back over there and try to pull that bartender."

I took a few steps away from her because I knew if I didn't things were only going to escalate.

"Have fun with her. I hope your dick falls off." Brandy hissed at me.

Chapter 6

Omari

I was the type of nigga who hated confrontation, I always tried to avoid the shit, I blamed the libra in me. I took a seat back at the barstool and rubbed my hands over my face. The bartender who name I still didn't know was on the other end of the bar serving new customers.

"Boss man thanks for tonight, we enjoyed ourselves," a few of my employees told me before they left out.

I looked around just to see how many were still drinking but only saw less than ten. I spotted Brandy and noticed that she was sitting and talking to one of my best realtors on the team. His name was

Jimmy, I watched her flirt with him for a few moments before I turned my attention back to the bartender who was walking over towards me.

"You look stressed, let me buy you a drink."

I squinted my eyes at her.

"Why are you being nice all of sudden?"

"I saw what happened with you and that girl. You really shouldn't go around playing with a bitch heart, we can be ruthless if we are fucked over."

I popped open my Coors light that she had passed me and took a sip of it.

"I don't play with bitches. You got it all wrong about me."

"How so? Tell me how you are different than all the other men who have come in here and have tried to get with me."

I took a deep breath and stared at her for a moment.

"You want the truth?"

"Yes, nothing but the fucking truth."

"I have always been a good man and have treated every girl I been with like she a fucking queen, but things changed for me once I fell in love with my ex. She made a complete fool of me and betrayed me. I took me a very long time for me to even talk about it, it still pains me two years later that she could have done me like she did. I put my all into our relationship only for her to be playing me the whole time. I'm not going to lie, I'm scorn over all the shit and promised myself to never fall in love."

"So do you think that gives you the right to fuck with other bitches and lead them on to believe it can be something more?"

"I never lead anyone on. They know exactly what they are getting themselves into when they meet me. I lay all the cards out on the table."

"Wow, so you tell them, you ain't looking for love, you just want to fuck?"

"Yes, I tell them that, but not that damn bluntly."

She laughed.

"Well, apparently she didn't get the memo."

"Who are you talking about, you mean Brandy?"

"Whatever her name is, she was pissed like ya'll had something going on."

"If we did, why do you care?"

"I don't care, I'm just proving a point."

"What's the point you trying to prove?"

"That you are just like everyone else."

I sat there in disbelief as she walked away from me.

No matter how hard I tried, I couldn't stop thinking about the sexy bartender. I was intrigued by her and wanted to get to know her. I had no clue how this was going to be possible when she had been so closed off towards me. She was different than anyone that I had ever met and that was what I was attracted to. She wasn't fake, at least I didn't get the impression that she was. She was real, blunt, and very opinionated. I was willing to do whatever just to get her attention.

I could barely concentrate on my work as my mind went into overdrive on how I was going to get her. Going back to the bar was the only option that I had. I only prayed that she hadn't lied to me about her shift that she worked. I was determined that later tonight, I was going to head over there to buy me a drink. Hopefully, if I was lucky, I would see her, and we could go from there. I was just about to head out to get me some lunch when I spotted Brandy hugged up with Jimmy. He had his hand placed over her ass as he whispered something into her ear.

Brandy must have felt someone watching because she looked me dead in the eye. Our eyes locked together for only a split second before she rolled her eyes at me. Yeah, the bitch was pissed but I didn't give a fuck. When I think back to it, she brought this shit on herself. She was the one who had come on to me, I was minding my own damn business. She threw herself at me. What nigga was going to turn down some free head?

She didn't even give me time to let her know that I wasn't looking for a fuck buddy.

I shook my head as I headed towards my car and hopped inside. If I could have gone back and done something over, letting Brandy suck my dick wouldn't have been one of them, I would have told her ass hell no.

I had faith that everything was going to work out for me because Brandy had already made it known that she had her sights on Jimmy. I didn't care who she fucked as long as she left me alone. I wanted all my focus to be on one thing and that was to get between that sexy ass bartender milk chocolate thighs.

The last thing I wanted was a man. I had just been fucked over by Ricco and wasn't about to let anyone ever get close to me again. I still couldn't believe that he would throw everything that we had away for some young ass thot. My ego was bruised because I thought I had Ricco wrapped around my finger, I guess I had been wrong.

Even though I had whopped both of their asses and had destroyed his little bitch apartment they both decided not to press charges. I already knew that his little hoe probably wanted to get Bambi and I both locked up but Ricco must have told her ass to leave the shit alone. He knows he had fucked me over and had known there was going to be consequences to his actions.

Right now, I was at the point in my life where I just wanted to forget I even fucked around with him in the first place. I went about my life and acted as if nothing had happened but deep down inside, I was crying out from the pain of being cheated on by the man whom I loved with all my heart and soul. I never wanted to feel this pain ever again.

I continued to go to work every single day and always tried to stay busy so I didn't have to think about what had happened, but the feelings were so strong that I still had a hard time blocking it all out.

Here I was standing in the hair salon doing one of my client's hair while I listened to Plies on my earphones. I wasn't in the mood to listen to the daily gossip that normally was held at the salon that I worked at. I wanted to be left alone with my own thoughts.

It had only been a few days, so the heartbreak was still fresh. My mother always used to tell me in order to get over a heartbreak without hardly feeling any of it was to get another man to take my mind off things.

Men were the last thing on my mind, but I still couldn't seem to stop thinking about the nigga that I had met at Snapper's Lounge. I didn't even know his name, but it was something about him that had me drawn to him from the moment we laid eyes on each other. Even though I was rude as hell to him, he still was determined to make conversation with me. I wasn't ready to be with a man emotionally, but I had needs and my pussy was crying out the entire time that he was near me. I highly doubt that I ever saw him again, but at least I knew that even though my heart was cold, my pussy still was working.

I did close to four heads that day before I clocked out. I picked me up a salad from Wendy's on my way home but only ate about two bites before placing it in the fridge for later. I could barely eat these days even though I knew I had to. Just the thought of him telling this hoe that he was going to leave me for her really shook me to my soul.

I laid my head down on my pillow and closed my eyes. I needed just a little nap because I had to mix drinks later that night.

His hands caressed my body as he slid his tongue into my mouth. We kissed for only a few moments before he picked me up and laid me on the ground. The sun blurred my vision for only a moment before he shielded the sun with his dark chocolate body. He ran his hands through my long hair just before he placed a gentle kiss on my forehead.

"You're so fucking beautiful, I can stare at you all day," he whispered to me.

The singing of the birds and gentle breeze of the wind made this moment feel so damn romantic. Here I was laying on the ground which was covered with flowers while he lightly caressed my body.

I squeezed my eyes shut when he slid his hand between my thighs and pushed them apart. He pulled up my summer dress and slid my yellow thongs off just before he began to caress my love box with his hand. I moaned softly just as he slid a finger into my honey pot.

"Shittt," I heard myself cry out as he fingered me.

I nearly lost my mind when he placed his mouth on my clit. He licked and sucked on my pearl tongue until I filled his mouth with my sweet nectar.

The sound of my alarm going off is what woke me from the dream. It was time for me to get my ass up and head to my night job. I wiped the sleep from my eyes but was still trying to grasp why I had such a sexual dream about the man who I had only just met once. Yeah, he was fine as hell, but damn, he wasn't that fine to the point that I was going to dream about him. I rubbed my hands through my tangled hair and headed into the bathroom so I could shower and get myself ready for that night. As I took care of my hygiene my mind began to wander off yet again back to the sexy man from the bar.

The nigga was fine as hell, and apparently single. He wasn't trying to commit due to him being hurt by a trifling ass bitch and I wasn't trying to fall in love with no other man after Ricco did me the way he did me. He had fucked it up for all men, but even though I hated seeing myself being in another relationship that didn't change the fact that my pussy was aching for his touch will my brain told me something different.

All I wanted was just sex and how he was talking that was all he was willing to give a bitch anyway.

After I was dressed, I stared at myself in the mirror for a few moments before heading out of the bathroom. I grabbed my keys and headed out of the house. I pulled up at the bar about ten minutes later and stepped out. I headed inside to get prepared for the nightly crowd when I spotted someone sitting at the bar. As I got closer, I froze. I wasn't expecting to see Ricco there. If I wouldn't have been at work, I would have hit his ass upside the head with a bottle.

"Why are you here?" I asked Ricco as I walked over to the bar to clock in.

"Look, I just wanted to come over to tell you that I'm sorry about how things went down. I never wanted to hurt you."

"You never wanted to hurt me, but was fucking another bitch behind my back. When were you going to tell me about her?" I asked aggressively.

Ricco became silent.

"Yeah, like I thought, you were going to continue to fuck with her and me until one of us found out about each other. You will never have a chance with me again. You fucked up when you stepped out on me."

"I didn't come here to fuss with you. I just want you to know that I'm going to always love you."

I cut him off mid-sentence and told him to shut the hell up. I honestly wasn't in the mood to hear his lies.

Ricco became quiet and stared into my eyes.

"Will you ever forgive me?" he asked.

I stopped what I was doing and looked at him for a few moments.

"You want my forgiveness?"

"Yes," he responded emotionally.

"Well, it will be a cold day in hell before I give you that."

Ricco stood there like I had slapped his ass in the face. If this nigga thought for one second I was going to forgive him then he was sadly mistaken. He was dead to me.

"You know, she wanted to press charges for destroying her apartment," but I begged her not to do the shit.

"You are the reason she got her ass whooped and her apartment trashed. You put her ass in danger when you were sneaking around with her. You better be glad I didn't kill her ass."

Ricco stood at me with his eyes wide open.

"I made a mistake, I fucked up," Ricco admitted.

"Yeah, you fucked up but there is nothing that you can do or say to make me forget or forgive you for breaking my heart. Now get the fuck out of my face, I'm trying to make my coins."

I saw nothing but pain in his eyes, but I didn't give a fuck. He brought this shit on himself.

"Can I at least finish getting my things out the apartment."

"I packed everything that belonged to you. There is no coming back to my apartment. It's over. Now do me a favor and tell your new bitch that she can have you."

Ricco was just about to grab me, but I walked away from his ass and went into the back. I had shit that I needed to be doing and playing games with Ricco wasn't one of them.

Chapter 8

Yvonne

I was minding my own damn business and mixing drinks when I looked up and spotted him. My heart skipped a beat and I quickly began to wonder what in the hell was wrong with me. Even though I was irritated as hell from Ricco popping up on my job, just seeing him seemed to make me get out of that funk. He walked over to me and took a seat in front of me.

I passed one of the customers his drink and began to fidget as I tried to make myself busy.

"How are you doing beautiful?" he asked me sweetly.

Instead of being rude like I did before I decided that I was going to be nicer.

"I'm doing okay, just agitated."

"What about?" he asked me calmly.

I ignored his question and asked him if he wanted something to drink.

"Yeah, I will take a Coors Light."

I grabbed his beer and gave it to him before I started busying myself with wiping down the counter. He placed his hand on mine and that's when I felt my stomach flip upside down. I snatched my hand from under his and gave him a weak smile.

He stared at me with a crooked grin before asking me why I was so tensed.

I bit down on my bottom lip and stared at him.

"I'm not going to spill my problems out, stop being so nosy," I told him.

"I'm not trying to pry, just making sure you good," he told me.

I only nodded my head at his comment as Bambi walked over towards me.

"I hope we get off early, I'm in need of some dick," Bambi, joked.

The tension that was in the air disappeared. Everyone laughed. I mean Bambi, could make anyone feel better. I swear she knew how to cheer me up when I was upset about some shit.

Her nigga and her had been together for over six years and they were still madly in love. I sort of envied what she had, but I knew deep in my heart that one day I was going to find the one for me.

"We got about two more hours and you can head your horny ass home," I told her.

Bambi giggled before she spotted a customer and went to take their order.

"Never mind her, that's the bestie. Her mouth is reckless."

"Ain't nothing wrong with that," he replied.

"If you don't want to tell me what's bothering you, then at least tell me your name."

"What's your name first?" I asked him curiously.

"My name is Omari. I'm thirty-five, I'm the CEO of Henderson Relator Agency."

I stood there with my mouth hung open. This nigga was successful and here he was trying to get to know me.

"It's your turn. Give me a little info on you. I already know you beautiful, so what else can you tell me."

I smirked before finally giving him what he was asking for.

"My name is Yvonne, I'm twenty-nine. I have no kids, I work here at night, and work at a hair salon during the day."

"Wow, you have two fucking jobs?" Omari asked in a shocked voice.

"Yes, I'm self-sufficient."

"Damn, I see that shit, you're grinding, I'm just stunned. I have never met a beautiful female who works two jobs."

"Well, here I am. I wasn't raised to depend on a nigga for shit. I work for what I want."

"How do your boyfriend feel about this?"

I stopped what I was doing and stared at him.

"What boyfriend?"

"Oh, I assumed you had a man. You too sexy to be single."

"I just got out of a relationship."

Omari took a sip of his beer and stared a hole in my face. He wanted the back story of my ex, I decided to tell him since he had told me about his ex when we first met.

"I was with him for two years, I recently found out he was cheating on me, so I left his ass."

"Damn, you didn't take him back?"

"Nope, I'm not like all these other bitches, once you fuck up with me it's a wrap."

"Do you still love him?"

"It just happened a few days ago, so yeah, I'm hurt about it, it's still raw and shit, I still love him even when I don't want to."

"Time will heal all wounds, but I know a quicker way to get over him."

"What will that be?" I asked him as I leaned over towards him.

"Getting you a new nigga and getting some new dick. You will forget about that lame ass nigga. He was dumb as hell to cheat."

"You believe fucking a new nigga will make me forget him?" I asked.

"Let me rephrase that. If you fuck on me, I will make you forget that lame ass nigga."

"Damn, your dick that fucking good to make a bitch forget their ex?"

"I have some powerful dick baby."

"I'm good on getting dicked down, I will just do the old fashion

way and let time work its magic."

Omari bit down on his lip as he undressed me with his eyes.

"All I need is an hour with you and your problem will be solved."

I rolled my eyes and laughed at his comment.

"Sex doesn't cure everything."

"It cures most things and a broken heart is at the top of the list."

"If you say so," I muttered.

"I'm honestly sorry that he fucked you over like he did, them

type of niggas just going to sweet talk you, come back to you, and

do it all over again."

"Trust I already know, I kicked him out and made it very clear

that we are over with."

Omari seemed as if he was impressed by my actions.

"Damn, you don't play any games, do you?"

"When it comes to my heart, I don't play around with that."

Omari nodded his head and took the last sip of his beer.

"You want another one?" I asked him.

"Nah, I'm good. I'm just going to sit here until you get off."

"Why are you waiting around for me to get off?"

"Since we first met last time, I can't stop thinking about you."

I was speechless because all I could think about was the nasty dream that I had about him earlier. The fact that he felt the same was was astonishing.

Even though Omari was fine as hell, I felt like it was best for me to keep my distance from men. Fucking did seem tempting, but I didn't even want to go there, I wasn't yet ready, at least I thought I wasn't ready."

"Look, I'm not going to make you do anything that you don't want to do. Honestly, I just want to chill nothing more."

I grabbed a shot glass and began drying it.

"I know what you are telling me and I'm going to say this. I'm not ready for nothing serious, I'm not looking for a relationship, fucking for me isn't something that I take lightly. I'm an emotional lover, fucking with me wouldn't be good for you."

"I'm not ready to be in a serious relationship either, you know my story and what I went through. All I want to do is show you a good time."

"Nah, I'm good on getting dicked down at the moment. I ain't got time to be catching feelings because then that's going to be a problem."

I was just about to walk away from him because I noticed a customer who needed his order taken. Omari grabbed me by my hand which stopped me in my tracks.

"No sex will be involved if you're not ready. Let's just chill."

"I will think about it," I told him before I headed over to my new customer.

"Damn bitch, who that fine ass nigga you were talking to. I saw how ya'll were looking at each other. Ya'll looked like ya'll was about to fuck."

I laughed and waved Bambi off.

"He came in to get a drink when I was working the evening shift. I just found out his name is Omari."

Bambi beamed.

I could tell how she was staring at me that she was thinking of something mischievous to do.

"That man is too fucking sexy, if I didn't have my boo, I would love to fuck on him."

I swear Bambi had no filter, I wiped my eyes as tears from laughing at her as began to fall down my cheeks.

"I'm just saying boo, you can't be turning down dick. You single now bitch, you better start acting like you are."

As Bambi walked off, I turned back and there stood Omari, staring at me like I was the only bitch in the room. My whole body grew hot and my pussy started dripping. I wasn't going to lie, my body wanted him, but my mind told me fucking with him wasn't going to be good for my health.

As my shift came to an end, Bambi and I were heading out the door. My feet were aching and a bitch was exhausted.

Bambi and I were just about to head to our cars when Omari yelled out my name.

"Yvonne!"

Bambi and I turned around and that's when I spotted Omari jogging towards us. It was damn near two in the morning and this nigga was still out and about.

"You must thought I was lying when I told you I was going to wait until you got off."

Just when I was about to speak, Bambi cut me off and introduced herself to him.

"I'm her bestie. My name is Bambi. What's your name?" Bambi asked him as she shook his hand.

"I'm Omari, I'm just a regular ass nigga trying to get to know her friend."

Bambi giggled and I rolled my eyes. She thought this shit was funny.

"Well, my bestie been through a lot give her a little time, I'm sure she will come around. But, don't hurt her, because if you do, you going to have to answer to me. I ain't got shit to lose, I stay ready to fuck some shit up."

Omari raised both hands to let her know that he wasn't a threat.

"I ain't trying to hurt Yvonne, she will be safe with me"

I nearly choked after I heard him say that shit. I was standing there clutching my bag and listening to these knuckleheads talk about me like I wasn't even there.

Omari finally turned his attention back to me and had the nerve to ask me if I wanted to slide on over to his crib. I eyed this nigga up like he was crazy.

"Um, its two in the damn morning. I'm not going anywhere but to my damn bed. I'm tired and my feet ache."

"I know you've had a long day at work tonight, but if you come over I promise you that you can rest in peace and I will even massage your feet."

"Damn," Bambi, whispered under her breath.

"Nah, I'm good on that. You just trying to get me over to your crib so you can try to fuck on me."

"What the hell? That is not my intentions. I just want to get to know you. I'm not trying to fuck you, I promise you that. If you get there and you want to leave then, by all means, I will let you go, but at least attempt to come over and chill with my ass."

I stared over at Bambi and she gave me that look like, bitch you better take your ass over there and have some fun.

I looked back at Omari and decided it was best to decline his office.

I could tell by how he looked at me that he was hurt, but I was doing what was best for me.

Just when I was about to slide into my vehicle Omari grabbed me. Our eyes connected and I felt as if my soul was on fire.

"Don't push me away. Don't fuck this up for either one of us. I'm not trying to fuck you if you don't want me to. All I want to do is treat you how you deserve to be treated. You said your last man fucked you over, well let me prove to you that I'm different. Follow me home, I was only going to run you a nice bubble bath, massage your feet, and send your ass to bed. Nothing more will be going on unless you want it to."

Even though my brain told my ass to hop in the car and pull off, another side of me was curious about him. Instead of thinking so hard on the subject I decided to follow his ass to his crib.

I gave Bambi a big hug and promised that I was going to text her in the morning to let her know how things went.

"Gone and get you some new dick boo and watch he go crazy over you," Bambi whispered in my ear.

"This nigga ain't about to get no pussy play here. He ain't trying to get serious about no bitch, he just wants to fuck, at least that's what he told me when we first met."

"And you ain't trying to get serious about no nigga, you just want to be fucked. Sounds like ya'll are perfect for each other."

"Maybe you're right," I agreed with Bambi.

I waved Bambi bye as she slid into her car and sped off.

"Are you ready to head out?" Omari asked.

I nodded my head at him.

"Lead the way," I told him just before I hopped into my car.

We pulled up at his spot fifteen minutes later and I followed him inside. When I first walked in, I stood there in disbelief. Even though his crib was a bachelor pad, I was shocked at how clean it was.

"You can take a look around if you want to. It's a two bedroom with one bath. I'm about to go get us something to drink."

I walked around his living room and looked at a few of his family pictures of him as a kid with his family.

"Is this your mother?" I asked him as he passed me a glass of red wine.

"Yes, she died a few years back of Cancer. We were very close."

"I'm sorry about that," I replied sadly.

"Don't be, I know she is in a better place," he told as he sipped

his drink.

As I sipped my wine, he headed down the hallway.

"Where are you going?" I asked him questioningly.

"I'm running you a hot bubble bath like I promised you."

I couldn't help but smile as I followed him. The scent of the

peach bubble bath filled my nose as I took another sip of my wine.

"This wine is so fucking good," I told him.

"I'm glad you like it."

After the tub was good and filled up with bubbles and water, he

walked over to me and told me to get undress. He took the wine

glass from my hands and placed it on the side of the tub.

"Once you get in the tub and get comfortable let me know, I will

come back in and massage your little feet."

"Okay," I whispered.

I waited until he had closed the door behind him before I slid out of my clothes and slid my way into the tub. I closed my eyes and softly moaned under my breath as the water caressed my tired body. I laid back in the tub and took a sip of my wine before placing it back.

After my body had relaxed and I had soaked for a good minute, I decided to call out for Omari to come in so I could get my foot massage like he had promised me.

"Omari, I'm ready for my massage!" I yelled out.

A few moments later, Omari came into the bathroom dressed in a pair of basketball shorts with a white t-shirt. The nigga was looking so fucking fine as he walked over to me. He had my pussy tingling, but I refrained from letting Omari know what his effect had on me.

I moaned softly as his strong hands began to massage my feet.

"Damn, if massaging your feet make you moan like that, I can't wait until I hear you moan when I fuck you."

"Boy hush, you ain't getting no pussy from me."

He chuckled.

"Maybe not tonight, but I will eventually."

I rolled my eyes at him and continued to let him do his thing. I was grateful that he had put a lot of bubbles in my bath because it covered all my private areas. I already knew, if he spotted anything on my body, he was going to want to fuck on me. I didn't come here to give up the pussy.

After he had massage both of my feet, I thanked him and told him that I was ready to get out of the tub. He grabbed me a big towel from the closet and sat it on top of the toilet before he walked out of the bathroom.

"I found you something to wear of mine for tonight when you get out just come into my bedroom."

I wrapped the towel around my naked body as soon as I stepped out the tub. My mind began to race as I tiptoed to his bedroom. This nigga thought he was slick, he was telling me to come into his bedroom knowing that I was naked just to fuck me. I laughed inside because I should have known better than to bring my ass over to his crib, I guess deep down inside, I wanted to fuck him too.

When I stepped into the bedroom he wasn't there, but a pair of his basketball shorts and a t-shirt was laying on his king-sized bed.

I dropped my towel and hurried to put them on before he came out of nowhere and scared my ass. I called out his name a few times before I realized he was in the second bedroom.

"What are you doing in here?" I asked him.

"Just fixing your bed up so you can get you some sleep. It's almost four in the morning. It's time for you to close your eyes and get some rest."

"I was tired as hell, but I didn't know if sleeping in such a strange place was a good idea."

"I think I may just head home. I live nothing but ten minutes away."

"No, you're going to stay here for tonight. It's way too late for you to be out driving. You can leave in the morning, I'm not holding you hostage, you have this whole room to yourself. I'm not going to bother you."

After he had finished making up my bed, he walked over to me and placed a kiss on my forehead.

"Did the bath and massage help?"

"Yes," I choked out.

Just being so close to him had my body reacting. I was lucky that I had on big clothes and he couldn't see that my nipples were erect.

"Have a good night," he whispered into my ear before closing the door behind me.

I flipped off the lights and slid under the covers. I laid there in bed as I heard him walk around the apartment. A few moments later everything got quiet. Tonight had been beautiful and there was no sex involved. He had truly treated me like a Queen.

I closed my eyes with a smile on my face before drifting off into a deep sleep.

I woke up the next morning and headed down the road to McDonald's and ordered Yvonne and me some breakfast with two cups of coffee. I was lucky that I didn't have to wait in line for a long ass time to get my food. As I headed back to the house I couldn't stop thinking about Yvonne and how she had shocked me by coming home with me.

I caught hell trying to persuade her to come to my crib and to be honest, I still thought she was going to turn my ass down. I was determined to get her alone and I had succeeded. Now I didn't have a clue where we stood. She seemed to enjoy herself last night and I didn't pressure her to do anything that she didn't want to do. I was the perfect gentlemen and had sent her to bed untouched.

I laid in bed most part of the morning, not really being able to sleep. She was only a few feet away and I wanted nothing more to slip into her room and slide between her thighs. I could tell that Yvonne was different then all the other bitches I had fucked with. She wasn't eager to fuck on me, instead, she was reserved and nonchalant about the whole situation. This was like a challenge to me and I was determined to change her mind about who she thought I was at a person. Yvonne didn't have the qualities of a hoe, so I wasn't about to treat her like one. Instead, I was going to treat her like the very Queen that she was. I wanted to make love to her, not just fuck her.

I wanted her to feel safe with me and I wanted her to trust me. Yes, I knew this was going to be a hard task, but I was willing to work my ass off to accomplish this goal.

I pulled up at my crib a few moments later and grabbed the bag and two coffees. I stepped into the house to find that everything was just like I had left it. That only meant one thing, Yvonne was still sleeping in the back room. I sat the food down and headed to the room that Yvonne was sleeping in. I stopped in my tracks when I heard soft moans. Curiosity got the best of me and I slowly walked over to her half-cracked door and spotted Yvonne fingering herself. She was so deep into what she was doing that she had no clue that was standing out there watching her. I stood there and couldn't tear my eyes away no matter how hard I tried. My dick grew big and the constant sound of her moaning was making me want to slide into her bedroom and blow her back out.

Instead of letting her reach her peak, I decided to bust in on her. She was about to let her catch a nut unless I was going to catch one with her. If she was that damn horny, she could have easily asked me to break her off.

Yvonne sat up in bed and tried to cover her private area, but it was too late, I had already seen exactly what she looked like.

"What the hell! You could have knocked," Yvonne said with attitude.

"And you could have closed your door. I came to tell you that I got breakfast in the kitchen, if you hungry you need to come to eat while it's hot."

"I will be there in a few moments, just give me five more minutes."

"Cool," I told her before closing the door behind her.

As I ate my sausage and cheese McMuffin I couldn't take the image of Yvonne masturbating. The sight of her burned an image in my brain and it wasn't anything I could do to turn it off.

When Yvonne walked into the kitchen she was dressed in her old clothes that she had worn to my house and she had her hair pulled up into a messy bun. I watched her as she pulled out a chair and dug into her food.

"Thanks for the food," she told me between bites.

"You're welcome."

I took the last bite of my sandwich and started sipping on my coffee. I almost fucked around and burnt my tongue off when she asked me how long I had watched her.

"I saw enough," I told her truthfully.

She nodded her head at me before sipping her coffee.

I had never been the type of nigga to beat around the bush, I was blunt and didn't give a fuck what anyone thought when I spoke my mind. I had learned at an early age if I wanted something I had to speak up and grab the shit. I wanted Yvonne and the fact that I knew she wanted me to, was what drove me to the point of confronting her.

"Yvonne, you're grown. Let's not play around with one another. I know you want me, I knew from the moment we met the first time at the bar that you were attracted to me, you really ain't that good at hiding her feelings, even if you think you are. I saw you masturbating, and I already know you were probably thinking about me the whole time. I would have let you had that release that you desperately was craving, but nah, if I can't get any release then neither can you. Don't act like you scared of me, I ain't going to hurt you, all I want to do is make love to your body and treat you like the Queen that you truly are. We both want each other, it's time we both admitted it."

Yvonne looked like I had slapped her in the mouth. She stared at me with her big pretty eyes and once she noticed that I was speaking some real shit, that's when she finally broke.

"I'm not going to lie, I do want you, but you ain't good for me."

"What makes you say that?" I asked her curiously.

"We both been hurt, we can't offer each other nothing but our bodies. I'm far from dumb, I know what sex can do. If we take it there, there will be no going back Omari. Sex is all good and fun until emotions get in the way, and don't sit there and tell me that you just want to fuck and don't want anything else. Nigga, don't lie to me. A nigga ain't going to go through this much for just some pussy, you already feeling something a little deeper down inside and it's only going to grow when I break you off some of this pussy."

I sat there speechless because even though Yvonne was acting reluctant about us fucking I actually was beginning to understand the reason why. I stood up, walked over to here and embraced her in a tender hug before placing a kiss on her forehead. Everything that she had said was the truth. I dreaded falling in love and not being able to have control over my feelings. Sex was just something I did to get a release and get a little satisfaction without feeling anything, but as I stared down at Yvonne, I knew what we shared was different. I wanted her, I wanted to get to know her, I didn't want to let her go, and whenever we did seal the deal and actually come together to have sex, I knew deep down I wouldn't want to let her go. I had a choice to make at that very moment. I had the option of walking away from Yvonne so I could pursue someone I wasn't so attracted to, or I could stay right where I was at and just see where things took us.

No matter how much my brain told me to run, the chemistry that Yvonne and I shared was stronger.

"Yvonne you're so right, we both been hurt, and this chemistry that we have for each other is something that neither one of us have experienced. We can both walk away and save each other the pain and heartache if this fails or we can stay right here and make a go for it."

Yvonne smiled at me before placing a kiss gently on my lips.

"I'm not going anywhere."

"Me neither," I responded back to her before sliding my tongue into her mouth.

Some people didn't believe in love at first sight or what it meant

to be drawn to someone. Some just didn't understand the power of

chemistry and where it could lead. Sometimes the attraction could

be so strong that it wasn't any point in fighting it. I always told

myself that I wasn't ever going to be with just one woman but once

I laid my eyes on Yvonne, she was a constant fixture in my life. I

wanted to fight the urge of wanting more than just a quick nut, but

I gave up the fight early on. I had lost this battle, but I knew it was

the right thing to do.

We both had been fucked over and hurt in our previous relationship, we both understood what love could do if you fell in love with the wrong person, but I was ready to move on with my life and find out what could happen when you fall in love with the right person. I was eager to learn where Yvonne and I were headed and how far we were going to go with one another. She was different than all the rest of the bitches that I had met along the way who I had fucked with. Yvonne knew the suffering that I had experienced and had been through her own troubles with her previous relationship, we both knew all too well what it felt like to be hurt, and I was confident that we wouldn't do that to one another.

I was at work in deep thought when my cell began to vibrate. I grabbed my phone out my pocket and my whole face lit up when I noticed it was Yvonne messaging me.

Yvonne: Hey bae, send me your address to your job. Maybe we can have lunch today.

Omari: 110 South Houston Lake Rd. What are you bringing for lunch?

Yvonne: I got a taste for some tacos.

Omari: Okay, that sounds good to me. When are you going to head over here?

Yvonne: In another hour.

Omari: Cool, see you then boo.

Yvonne and I haven't even fucked yet and she already had me on this emotional high. Just knowing that she wanted to come over and have lunch with me had me deep in my feelings. We were really going to do this, we were really going to try to make something happen of this chemistry that we both shared for one another. I still couldn't believe it until she walked through my office door an hour later.

She was dressed in a pair of skin-tight blue jeans, a black and white shirt with some designs on it, with a pair of black sandals. We embraced in a hug just before we kissed each other lightly on the lips.

"I didn't think I was going to see you this soon," I told her seriously.

"What makes you say that? You must think I was going to change my mind."

"Yep," I stated.

"Well, I meant what I said. The question is have you changed your mind?"

"Of course not, I'm all in."

"Good," she laughed.

We ate our tacos and joked around until a knock came at the door. To be honest, I wasn't expecting it to be Brandy since she rarely came into my office, but I guess someone must have told her that I had someone in my office because here she stood.

She was dressed in a pair of black and red shorts, with black converses, with a red plain shirt. She had her long hair pulled pack in a low ponytail and her lips were painted red.

I had been avoiding her since she had tried to make a scene at the bar. I honestly didn't have time for any drama. She was one bitch that I hated I had stepped over the line with.

"What can I do for you, Brandy?" I asked her professionally.

Brandy glanced over at Yvonne and rolled her eyes at her.

My heart began to race and I quickly said a silent prayer that Yvonne didn't react. I exhaled when Yvonne smirked at the bitch instead. She paid Brandy no fucking mind.

After Brandy noticed that she couldn't get a reaction out of Yvonne she decided to result to some drastic measures.

"I just wanted to bring in my internship paper so you can sign off on it," Brandy replied.

I reached out to grab the paper and that's when her hand brushed across mine. I snatched my hand away and focused my attention on filling out her paperwork.

After I had filled everything out, I handed it back to her and told her to enjoy her weekend.

"Thanks, Mr. Henderson, I just wanted to let you know that this week will be my last week of interning here. I asked my teacher to move me to another location."

I sat there in disbelief because I wasn't expecting to hear this.

"If you don't mind me asking, why did you want to leave? Don't you like it here?" I asked.

"Oh, yes, I love it here, but I asked to be moved because there is an office that is much closer to where I live that I can intern at as well. Plus, I felt it was only right that I left due to the little session

we had a week ago. I just don't want to cause you any problems."

I swear I wanted to throw Brandy across the room, that bitch

knew exactly what she was doing. She came in here to throw shots

at Yvonne because she was jealous and wanted me herself.

"Brandy, stop right there. Don't say anything more. Nothing

happened between us."

Brandy chuckled.

"Oh, but something did happen. If I can remember straight, I

sucked your dick right here in this very office. But I'm done with

the fuckery Mr. Henderson, I just wanted to let you know that I'm

leaving and if you ever want to hang out here is my number to

reach me."

I watched her in disbelief, as she scribbled down her number on a

sticky pad and stuck it to my desk.

"Enjoy the rest of your day, Mr. Henderson."

I sat their stone face as Yvonne stared at me.

"What did you do to her? You sure got that little bitch pressed."

"I met you, that's what happened. Fuck all these hoes, ain't no bitch better than you." I assured Yvonne.

Yvonne smirked before throwing the rest of our food away and hopping her fine ass on top of my desk.

"Prove to me that I'm the only one you want. I'm not with all that talk, I want some action."

She didn't have to tell me twice. I wasted no time pulling down her jean shorts and snatching off her thong. I didn't give a fuck that we were in my office, I had to have her ass right then and there. I wanted to at least taste her.

I slid her thighs apart and flicked my tongue around her clit before I slid a finger into her honey pot. She let out a soft moan as she laid back on top of my desk.

She squeezed her eyes shut as I stroked my finger into her wetness.

"Shit, that feels so fucking good," she cried out.

I licked and sucked on her clit as her pussy juices soaked my two fingers. I was determined to make her cum, when her moans began to get louder, I knew she was on the verge of reaching her peak. I flicked my tongue over her pearl one last time before her legs began to tremble and shake. As her cream spilled from out her love box, I made sure to suck every drop out her coochie. After her body had come down from her high, I helped her off my desk.

"Shit, that tongue don't fucking play. No wonder that bitch acting crazy," she muttered as she slid back on her clothes.

"I didn't give her any head, she gave me some head, instead. I can't afford to break every bitch off with this tongue and dick."

Yvonne squinted her eyes at me.

"Don't look like that at me, you the only one who going to be getting this tongue and dick," I told her.

"Right, I better be," Yvonne replied.

I shook my head at her and pushed her up against my desk before telling her just how good she had tasted.

"Believe me when I say, you all I want and need."

Yvonne didn't speak, she only nodded her head.

I understood the pain that Yvonne had experienced with her ex, I knew I was going to have to break down a shit load of walls, but I was willing to do all of that for her. I wanted her to be in my life and I was willing to cut off any and all bitches just to please her.

Chapter 12

Omari

After Yvonne had left my office, I sat there and decided it was time to think of something to let Yvonne know that I only had eyes on her. I wanted to romance her, so I thought why not buy her some roses and take her to dinner later that night.

I shot her a text and told her to send me her address. A few seconds later she sent me the information I needed. I also made sure to tell her to be dressed later that night because I was taking her out.

I didn't have time to be playing games, I was ready to take this shit to the next level. After getting a taste of her sweet pussy, I knew I had to lock her ass down. I wasn't about to let no nigga come in and scoop her ass up.

I breezed through work the rest of the day and was ecstatic when I spotted Brandy messy ass packing up her shit to leave. If she thought I was going to hit her ass up then she had another thing coming. That bitch was trying to ruin me just because she could. What these hoes failed to realize was they were the ones who put themselves in situations to be fucked over.

Brandy had come on to me, I could have told her ass no, but what nigga going to turn down getting their dick sucked? Ain't no nigga going to turn down that shit, but the hoe didn't give me any type of clue that she wanted more than to suck my dick. How was I supposed to know she was going to get out of control and feel like I was only going to be with her and fuck on her.

Oh hell nall, there is no way you can come at a nigga offering pussy and head and throw yourself at him the way she did and not expect to be used for your services. She didn't ask me if I had a bitch or where we stood, so I only assumed it was just something to do.

She had truly played herself trying to fuck up what I was trying to build with Yvonne. Just because I didn't want her didn't mean she wasn't going to find another nigga who was going to take her up on her offer. I said a silent prayer to the man above for protecting me from Brandy, because she could have really fucked me up if she wanted to.

I walked out of the office with a smile on my face. I hopped in my car and merged into traffic as I headed to the store to grab my baby some flowers. After purchasing her a dozen roses, I headed straight to my crib so I could shower and get ready for that night.

I looked at the clock and it was five in the evening. I shot Yvonne a text to let her know that I was going to be over there around seven to pick her up.

I sat the red roses on my kitchen table while I headed to the bathroom to take care of my hygiene. I stayed in the shower, for over forty minutes before I hopped out. I tore up my closet trying to find something to wear for that night. I finally decided to put on a pair of black jeans, a grey, and black shirt, with a pair of black and grey Nikes.

I sprayed on me some cologne, brushed my hair, and put on my jewelry. A nigga was finally dressed and I was beginning to feel nervous as hell. Honestly, I didn't know what to expect when I got over to Yvonne's house, I'm not going to lie, I was hoping that she wasn't a nasty ass chick who was pretty on the outside but didn't believe in cleaning up her crib. I grabbed my keys and her roses from off the table and headed out the door. I slid into my car and made sure to type in her address in Google Maps before I took off to her destination.

I pulled up at her crib ten minutes later and sat in the car for a few moments before getting out. I mean I wanted to check out the fucking neighborhood before I stepped out. You could tell a lot about a bitch from how she carried herself and how she kept her house. My heart began to race as I walked up to her apartment door and knocked. I knocked close to five times before she finally answered.

"I'm sorry, I was back there with my music up getting ready," she apologized as she stepped aside.

I passed her the roses that I had gotten for her and she quickly put them to her nose.

"Aww, you ain't have to do all this, but I love them so fucking much," she told me as she headed in the kitchen to put them in water. After she had taken care of the roses, she came back into the living room where she had left me at.

I took in my surroundings and exhaled when I noticed just how clean it was and how good it smelled.

"Damn nigga, I mean what the fuck wrong with you. That face you making got me wanting to smack your ass."

"I'm sorry, I just thought."

"What exactly did you think?" Yvonne asked.

"I've noticed that most bitches who look good and real sexy don't keep a clean house, I mean they be so nasty, I be wondering how they stay there."

Yvonne laughed so hard that she almost fell over.

"So you came over her just to see if I fit into this category."

I didn't say anything, so I guess that gave her the answer that she was looking for.

"Well, as you can see, I'm a neat freak. I'm not a nasty bitch."

"I see that you aren't."

Yvonne giggled as she headed back in the bathroom to finish getting dressed.

I sat down on her soft plush couch and grabbed the remote. I flipped through a few channels until I landed on a Fox movie. I was just about to get into the movie when Yvonne fine ass stepped in front of the T.V. She was wearing a tight black spandex dress that left nothing to the imagination. Her hair was pulled back from her face and her lips were painted purple.

"I'm ready to head out," she told me as she cut off the T.V.

I followed her out the door towards my car and made sure to be the perfect gentleman and hold the door for her.

"Awww, damn, you really going all out tonight," she joked.

"You have no idea," I told her.

"Where are we going to eat?" she asked me as she stared out the window.

"You will see."

We pulled up at the Logan's RoadHouse a fifteen minutes later. It was packed, but we managed to find us a decent parking spot.

"Damn, its lit in this bitch," Yvonne said as I helped her out the car.

After we had been taken to our seats, Yvonne and I laughed and talked about each of our days. It wasn't long before we started talking about the amazing head that I had given her.

Yvonne smirked as she placed her feet up against my dick.

I eyed her ass up because I knew she wanted the dick and probably was down to fuck right at that very moment.

"You so freaky I swear," I joked her.

"Don't nobody want no boring bitch," she told me as she stared at her menu.

When the waiter came to take our order, I could tell that he was checking Yvonne out just by how he was looking at her. I was a man, so I knew when a nigga was lusting after a bitch. I watched it as the shit played out. Yvonne flipped through the menu not really knowing what to eat, this gave the waiter the perfect opportunity to get her attention.

Next thing you know the waiter went over and beyond to help her find a good seafood meal.

She ordered the lemon herb chicken with rice. I ordered the grilled salmon and sent the waiter on about his business.

"Damn bae, you were rude as hell," Yvonne told me after the waiter had disappeared.

"Nah, I wasn't rude, that nigga better be glad I didn't punch his ass."

"What he do?" Yvonne asked with a confused look on her face

"Baby, he was checking you out and he was flirting with your ass super hard. I'm glad you weren't playing that nigga no mind, but he wasn't that much concerned with any of these other bitches around here with helping them order a meal."

Yvonne laughed.

"Baby, you over exaggerating. That waiter ain't my type."

"Well, you his type then," I muttered.

Yvonne rolled her eyes.

"Let's not go there, I just want to enjoy our meal and our time out together."

"I'm willing to make that shit happen," I told her gently.

Our meal came almost forty minutes later, everything was delicious, and we really enjoyed ourselves. After we had paid our bill, we headed out the door and slid into my car.

"I enjoyed tonight," Yvonne told me as I cruised towards her house.

"I'm glad you had a great time," I told her.

I cut on my radio and had it on a low volume so I could still hear her talk if she wanted to say something to me. Chris Brown poured out from the speakers. As Chris Brown music filled the car Yvonne took that time to start lightly stroking my dick.

My manhood instantly began to respond.

"Keep your eyes on the road baby, I'm about to give you the best head that you've ever had."

Yvonne wasn't lying when she said that shit.

She pulled my manhood out and wasted no time sliding it into her wet mouth. I groaned as she slurped and sucked on the head of my dick while she stroked me with her hand. It took everything in me to not wreck my fucking car. I was grateful when I spotted her apartment complex up the road. I pressed on the gas and swooped in. I parked in front of her apartment building and closed my eyes as I finally got the chance to enjoy her mouth.

I rubbed my hands through her long hair as she deep throated me. She was sucking my dick so good that she had my toes curling inside my shoes.

"Fuck. I'm about to cum," I groaned.

Yvonne didn't let up on her mouth skills, instead, she intensified them. Yvonne took my soul right from out my ass and swallowed every drop. She was nasty and I liked every bit of it.

Chapter 13

Yvonne

If this nigga thought I was about to let him suck my pussy and have me acting out my mind, then he had another thing coming. When I saw the look on Omari's face, I knew that my mouth had fucked his little head up. He picked me up and carried me into my apartment. I had my legs wrapped around his waist as he carried my ass to my bedroom.

We were so damn horny that we didn't even try to take off all our clothes. He pulled up my black spandex dress and snatched down on my black thongs. He hurried to unzip his black pants and pulled out his thick monster. He caressed it in his hands a few times before he slid between my thighs. His dick wasn't small at all, so when he slid into me, I gasped. I gripped my bedsheets as he dived into my wetness.

I wrapped my legs tightly around his waist as he gently began to stroke his manhood deep inside me.

We stared into each other eyes and kissed as he made love to me. His stroke game was A1 and his dick filled me up. I cried out his name as he sucked and licked on my neck while he continued to deep stroke me.

When my pussy had warmed up and had gotten use to his size, he slid out of me and placed me on top of him. I slid him inside me and cried out his name as he pulled me down on his chest. He smacked my ass a few times as he began to beat my coochie down.

I bit down on his neck as he slid his finger into my ass.

"Shit!" I yelled out as he continued to pound me.

He was fucking me so roughly that the bed board was pounding up against the wall.

I tried running from the dick, but Omari wasn't having that shit.

"I'm not done with you yet," he whispered into my ear as he held me tightly in his arms as he continued to fuck me.

When he was done, he slid out of me, and told me to stick my ass in the air. I placed my face into my pillow as he caressed my bootie.

I moaned out in pleasure as he started eating my ass as he played with my clit.

"Fuck," I cried out as I laid there not able to do nothing but take the tongue lashing that he was giving. He licked my ass and played with my clit until I reached my peak. As soon as I started creaming, he slid into me from the back and started slow grinding inside my love nest.

This nigga knew exactly what he was doing because he had me nutting back to back. He slammed into my love box a few more times before he spilled his seed into my love vessel. We disconnected ourselves from one another a few moments later. I laid on his chest and listened to his heartbeat while he played with my nipples.

"That was mind-blowing," he told me.

"Yes, you ain't lied. I don't think I'm going to be able to walk for a few days."

"I wasn't that hard on you, shid, that pussy was good as fuck, I wasn't about to let it go to waste. I wanted to get as much out you that I could." Omari admitted,

"Well, you did your thing. You got me hooked. Aint nobody ever fucked me like you did. I 'm not pressed for anybody but you."

"You just don't know how long I've been waiting to hear you say that," Omari admitted to me.

"You ain't pressed for a nigga, and I'm not pressed on finding another bitch, you all I need," Omari told me gently.

"As long as you promise to always be here, I will promise to always remain by your side," I told Omari softly.

He looked down at me and placed a kiss on my lips.

"Baby, you came into my life and turned it upside down. I went from not wanting to be in a relationship to us trying to see where this goes. After my ex hurt me the way she did I never wanted to love or go through that pain ever again, but once I met you, all that shit changed for me. I couldn't shake the feeling that I had for you and the scary part about it is, I didn't want to shake them. We both taking a risk with each other, but it's going to be worth it."

"Awww baby, I feel the same way. All I got to say is, you were right when you told me that I could easily get over my ex if I found someone else. I don't even think about my ex anymore and I have you to think for that. You were determined to fuck on me and I was determined to keep you away from me. Your love got me all shook up. You came in and shut some shit down," I told him as I caressed his chest.

"Now look at us, laying here in bed all naked and shit," Omari joked.

I closed my eyes as Omari began to stroke his hand through my hair.

"My perspective has changed. I wanted to just fuck you at first, but now I want so much more than that, now I want to love you."

"No more running, I'm ready to give you all of me," I replied to Omari in a gentle voice.

Omari placed a soft kiss on my forehead before the room grew still and sleep found both of us.

Connect With Me On Social Media

Subscribe to my mailing list by visiting my website: <u>https://www.shaniceb.com/</u>

- **Like my Facebook author page:** <u>https://www.facebook.com/ShaniceBTheAuthor/?ref=aymt_homepage_panel</u>

- **Join my reader's group on Facebook. I post short stories and sneak peeks of my upcoming novels that I'm working on** <u>https://www.facebook.com/groups/1551748061561216/</u>

- **Send me a friend request on Facebook:** <u>https://www.facebook.com/profile.php?Id=100011411930304&_nodl</u>

About The Author

Shanice B was born and raised in Georgia. At the age of nine years old, she discovered her love for reading and writing. At the age of ten, she wrote her first short story and read it in front of her classmates, who fell in love with her wild imagination. After graduating from high school, Shanice decided to pursue her career in Early Childhood Education. After giving birth to her son, Shanice decided it was time to pick up her pen and get back to what she loved the most.

She is the author of over twenty books and is widely known for her bestselling four-part series titled Who's Between the Sheets: Married to A Cheater. Shanice is also the author of the three-part series, Love Me If You Can, and three standalone novels titled Stacking It Deep: Married to My Paper, A Love So Deep: Nobody Else Above you, and Love, I Thought You Had My Back. In November of 2016, Shanice decided to try her hand at writing a two-part street lit series titled Loving My Mr. Wrong: A Street Love Affair. Shanice resides in Georgia with her family and her six-year-old son.

The day that Arianna said the words 'I Do' she knew she was

making a mistake. She didn't love Dontae but was forced to marry

him because her mother wanted her to (secure her bag) for her future. Unhappy and depressed Arianna confides in her best friend Jaleesa about her loveless marriage, hoping her best friend can help her in some way.

As Jaleesa listens to Arianna whine and complain about Dontae, she finds herself becoming infatuated with her best friend's man. He is everything that she ever wanted, and she wants him for herself.

Once Jaleesa learns that Arianna is planning to leave Dontae, she decides to make her move and seduce him, but the happily ever after that she expects to have with her best friends' man doesn't go as planned.

Will Jaleesa be able to get the man she always wanted, or will her heart be shattered to pieces?

I Wish You Were My Boo is a tragic love story that tells a story

of just how far someone will go for the sake of the four-letter word

L.O.V.E.

Karly McAdams believes she is living the perfect life with her longtime boyfriend Javier, but things take a swift turn when tragedy hits. With a broken heart and with the desperation to move on with her life, Karly decides to fly to Minnesota to spend Christmas with her family.

After arriving back to her hometown, her mother introduces her to a model named Lindsey Mitchell. Lindsey has been happily married to her husband Carter for five years. She loves her man from the bottom of her heart and believes he feels the same about her until she learns of his betrayal. With her heart shattered to pieces, she feels she has no one to lean on until Karly makes it clear that she can confide in her.

As Lindsey and Karly's friendship becomes stronger, a full-blown romance occurs that neither can ignore. As their love for each other deepens, Lindsey will eventually have to make a choice between her family and the love she has for Karly.

Will their love survive, or will it wither and die?

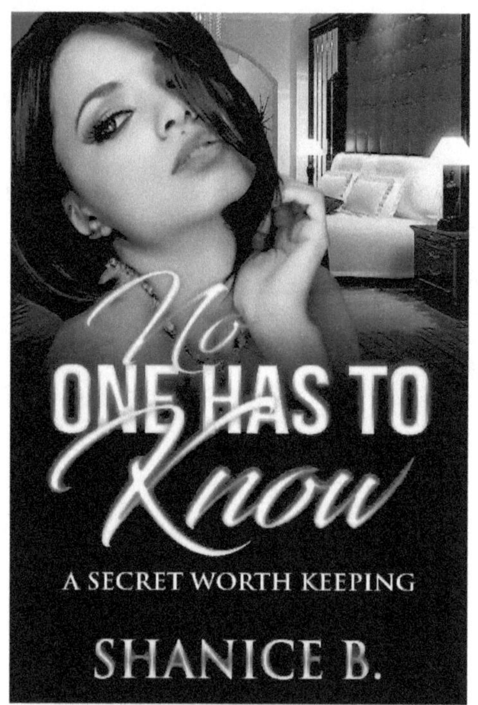

"Sometimes when you think you know a person, that's when you

learn that you never knew them at all."

Layla and her brother Lamar have always been close, but their

relationship soon starts to become rocky when Layla leaves her abusive boyfriend and moves in with Lamar and his girlfriend,

Promise. Lamar believes he's doing the right thing by stepping in

and helping his baby sister, but he soon will see that he has made a

fatal mistake.

When Promise learns that her boyfriend Lamar has cheated on

her, Promise feels as if her perfect world has been shattered right

before her eyes. As she tries to mend her broken heart, she soon

realizes that this will not be an easy task because she can't let go of

the pain of her man hurting her.

Promise and Layla are both having a hard time coping with their

love lives. They both feel as if they don't have anyone in their

corner to help them get through their difficult time. When they

realize that they're all each other have, an unlikely friendship

begins to bloom that is unbreakable.

After a sultry night involving too many drinks, their close

friendship turns into a hot steamy love affair.

They both know if Lamar ever finds out about their secret, all

hell will break loose, but they will soon conclude that what Lamar

don't know can't hurt him. Will Promise and Layla be able to keep

their love a secret or will Lamar recognize the red flags that

symbolize something just isn't right?

Meet Me In My Bedroom Volume 2 is a collection of erotic love

stories that will pull you in from the very first page. These erotic

stories are all hot steamy reads that are centered around romantic relationships. Volume 2 will make your panties wet and have you

begging for more. Read at your own risk. Enjoy!!!

Meet Me In My Bedroom will have you glued to your Kindle from the very first page.

These erotic love stories are steamy hot reads that are centered around romantic relationships.

Each love story is jaw dropping and will have you begging for more.

Read at your own risk. Enjoy!!

QUICK NOTE: This is a twelve-thousand-word erotic short story. If you are looking for something sexy and quick to read, then this will be the perfect read for you.

Heartbroken over her ex leaving her for another woman, Kira seems to not be able to shake her bruised ego. When Kira's best friend Shonda persuades her to have a girl's night out to take her mind off her heartbreak, Kira's life will forever be changed.

When Kira and Jacolby lock eyes on each other their burning desire and lust for one another is what they feel. Kira is FEENIN' for some dope dick and Jacolby just happens to be the man who is eager to please her inside and outside of the bedroom. Once Jacolby dicks her down, Kira finds herself falling for him hard and fast and there is nothing she can do about it but let it happen.

When Kira's ex magically reappears, she must make a decision. Will she go back to the man that has broken her heart or will she remain with the one man who has swept her off her feet and made

her feel things she has never felt before?